Six Dinner Sid
A Highland Adventure

INGA MOORE

Hodder
Children's
Books

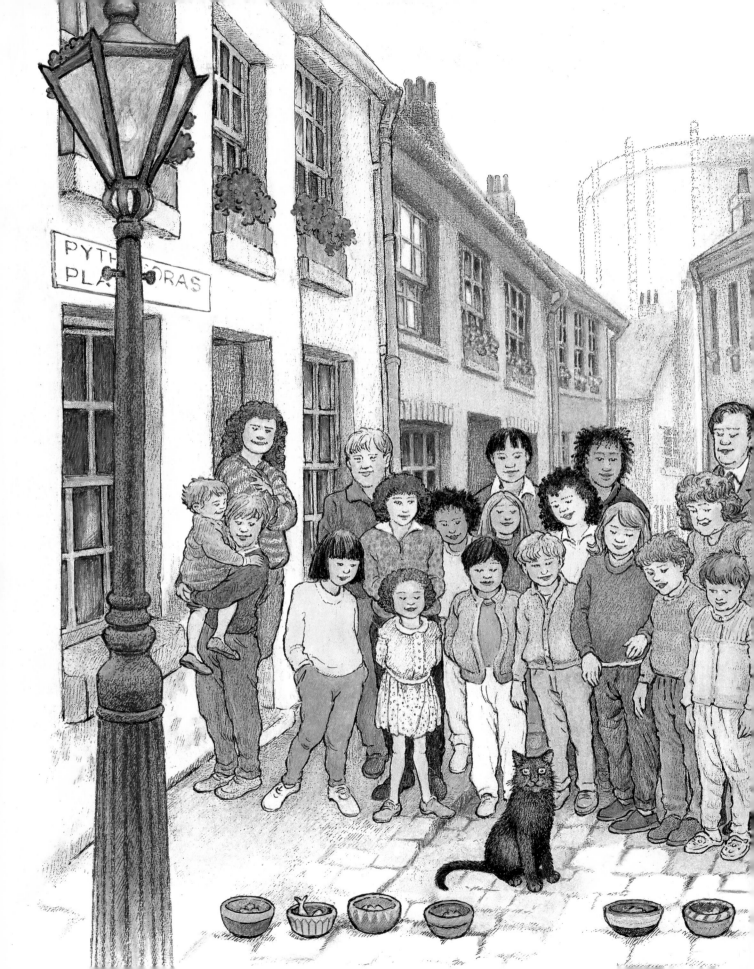

Sid ate no fewer than six dinners a day –
he wasn't called Six Dinner Sid for nothing!
He lived with six sets of owners in six houses,
numbers one, two, three, four, five and six
Pythagoras Place.

Apart from eating his six dinners there was nothing
Sid liked more than going in and out of his six houses.
Most of them were fairly easy to get into.

Others were a lot trickier,
requiring a good deal
of skill and agility.

Sid's owners would watch in amazement as he leapt from one window sill to another like a nimble mountain goat.

As for climbing, Sid was a natural
and he could always get himself
out of a tight spot.

He could always get himself
into one, too, as we are
about to find out!

Like most people, every year Sid's owners went on holiday.
But one year there was a problem.
For some reason, or another,
everyone wanted to go
at the same time.

'Who will feed Sid?' they said.
They couldn't send him to a cattery
because, at catteries, having six dinners
wasn't allowed. The people working there
were very strict about that sort of thing.

So in the end, Sid's owners decided that they would
all go on holiday together, taking Sid with them…

and when holiday time arrived
Sid was put into a travelling basket
and taken to the station to catch the train.

Sid had no idea where he was going but he hoped
it would be more or less like Pythagoras Place...

which was funny because,
in one way, it couldn't
have been *more* like
Pythagoras Place...

and, in another,
   it couldn't have been less!

Sid's owners had rented six
wooden cabins in
the Scottish Highlands.
Sid soon felt right at home.

Then he went into
the forest to explore.

He hadn't gone far
when a voice in a tree said,
'Halt, who goes there?'
'Sid,' said Sid.
'Well, hello Sid!'
said the voice,

and down from the tree
jumped the biggest tabby cat
Sid had ever seen.
'My name's Jock,' he said,
'and this is *my* forest.'

Jock, who was a Scottish wildcat,
offered to show Sid round.
As they went along, Sid told
Jock about his six dinners.
'Six dinners a day, eh?'
said Jock. 'My, my!'

Jock said, in the forest,
you could have as many
dinners a day as you liked.

'Of course,' he added. 'You have to catch them first!'
and he took Sid to a highland stream.

Swimming in the water was
Sid's favourite food – fish!

Jock showed Sid how to flip
one out with his paw.

But instead of flipping
the fish out of the water...

Sid flipped himself right
into it – SPLASH!

So Jock took Sid down to the loch and there,
lying asleep in a pool, was a lobster.
'You'll catch that right enough,'
said Jock.

But all Sid caught
was a big nip.
'YEEEOW!'
howled Sid.

As if this wasn't bad enough,
when Sid chased a rabbit…

and the rabbit ran down
a hole, so did Sid,
and he got stuck!

How those rabbits
laughed at Sid.
'Oh, well,' said Jock
digging him out,
'I suppose you *are*
only a city cat!'

On top of a crag, there was an eagle's nest.
Jock said his favourite food was eagles' eggs
 – at least he thought they were.
Actually he had never dared
to climb up to try one.
Sid couldn't think why –
the nest looked no harder
to get to than the skylight
in the roof of number 2,
Pythagoras Place.

So Sid decided to show Jock what
city cats were really made of.
'Come on, Jock!' he said,
and he led the way
up the steep crag.

They were almost at the top when,
oh, dear, the owner of the nest
spotted them!

The indignant
mother eagle
swooped down
to defend
her eggs.

Sid managed to hide
but Jock was not so lucky.

'Help!' he cried as the eagle grabbed him.

Sid took a swipe at the eagle. Then...

did he slip or did he jump? Sid never knew –

but somehow he found himself on the eagle's back.

The eagle dropped Jock
and with Sid on board
she flew up into the sky.
She twisted and turned
and looped the loop
trying to fling Sid off.

Sid was in an extremely tight spot
but he had been in tight spots before
and he managed to keep a cool head.

No matter how hard the eagle tried to fling him off,
Sid hung on.

He waited until
just the right moment.
Then, when the eagle was
closest to the ground,
he jumped. Sid knew
exactly how to land,
so he was not hurt.

'Phew!' said Jock.
'That was a near thing!
Well done, Sid!
You city cats are not
so bad after all!'

Jock saw Sid back to the cabins.
'Goodbye, Sid,' he said.
'Enjoy your six dinners!'

But with all that fishing and hunting and climbing
and flying around in the fresh highland air,
Sid had worked up quite an appetite...

He wasn't sure if six dinners
were going to be
enough tonight.

It was just possible
he would have to
find himself
a seventh.

Now *there* was a likely
looking campervan!